Story of a Clam

Story of a Clam

A FABLE
of Discovery & Enlightenment

Rebekah Alexander Dunlap
& Sir John Templeton

TEMPLETON FOUNDATION PRESS
PHILADELPHIA & LONDON

Templeton Foundation Press
Five Radnor Corporate Center, Suite 120
100 Matsonford Road
Radnor, Pennsylvania 19087

Scripture quotations are from *The Holy Bible*, King James Version.

Library of Congress Cataloging-in-Publication Data

Dunlap, Rebekah Alezander.
   Story of a clam : a fable of discovery & enlightenment /
Rebekah Alezander Dunlap & Sir John Templeton
        p. cm.
   Includes bibliographical references (p.).
   ISBN 1-890151-38-6 (pbk. : alk. paper)
      1. Clams—Fiction. I. Templeton, John, 1912– II. Title
PS3604.U55 S7 2001
813'.54—dc21   2001027017

Printed in Canada

01 02 03 04 05 06   10 9 8 7 6 5 4 3 2 1

Contents

Story of a Clam

Introduction

NGLISH PHYSICIST and mathematician Sir James Jeans once said that the universe was beginning to look, not like a great machine, but rather like a great thought. Much has been presented in a variety of forms about the power of the mind. And "mind" offers such a vast field for exploration! In the last fifty years, some of the world's best scientists have developed the Anthropic Principle, which examines whether the entire universe was developed in order to produce humans. Could it be possible that—at some time or some level—many other creatures might be so self-centered as to think that his species was the ultimate purpose of the universe because he was not yet able to become aware of more "advanced" or seemingly superior intelligences?

Most of us, on some level of consciousness, desire to

increase our awareness of life and help improve our lives, our thoughts and feelings, our environment. It certainly seems natural for us to want to be aware of what is going on within and around our world. However, as we become more willing to release the personal ego, we open the door to greater discovery. Truly, there is no place we can go where we are not bathed in the infinite sea of creativity. We are free spirits and our minds are not bound to anything unless we think we are.

In the motion picture *The Empire Strikes Back,* Luke Skywalker tries to lift a starfighter out of the muck and mire through the power of his thoughts—and fails. Yoda, the Jedi Master, lifts the starfighter easily. Luke stares at Yoda and says, "I didn't think it could be done." Yoda replies, "That is precisely why you couldn't do it." Yoda believed in and used the full power of the "Force," which could be described as the everywhere-present power of God that is within and all around us. If we are not enterprising and open to vast possibilities, our own doubts may defeat us as we struggle to lift ourselves out of the mire of earthly limitations.

Why would the lowly clam be chosen as the primary character for our allegory? Because Columbus Clam can be representative of our struggles for enlightenment and our resistance to change. Consider the possibility that every minute detail in Columbus Clam's adventure may not precisely correspond to a particular scientific theory or philosophical perspective. However, this story, taken as a simple analogy, may open some possibilities to a questing mind.

Are we often held back by the limitations of our own minds and the narrowness of our cultural experience? We see only dimly the vast unseen, and understand less of the *Creator* who lies behind all creation. We may think we have a fairly good understanding of life and "consciousness." But do we really? If we can imagine the events unfolding in this little reverie, can we also expand our thinking faculty and research the possibility that every atom may be included in infinite Divinity?

Even in this enlightened age of space travel and semiconductors, the early stages in each onward course of human development often occur through a shadowy twilight, which results in more diligent seeking. Occasionally, the light of illumination touches humankind and we are spurred forward, searching for answers, desiring more awareness of what lies beyond our immediate perceptions. Have we within us the power to rise above the confusions of our times? Can we be stronger than anything that may distress, grieve, or seem to limit us? So, let's affirm the truth of the great mystery of life with a conscious, deliberate, and powerful research of spiritual reality. Besides, have we not heard that *"with God all things are possible"*? (Matt. 19:26)——even the elevation and evolution of a lowly clam!

We live in a world of change, a world that can sometimes seem to be a stranger and more baffling place than we may have thought. It can certainly be filled with creative surprise, even to the point of generating sentient beings such as ourselves! As we consider the wonders our eyes behold, it is not difficult to sense something incredibly imaginative, purposeful, and powerful taking place. Perhaps in the future it will be possible to describe these wondrous phenomena in far more sophisticated scientific terms. But we are inclined to think that a full scientific description will still elude us, because the true definition will require knowledge of the infinite god of the universe, whose reality we only dimly perceive while he "holds in being" the universe.

So, Dear Reader, may you enjoy this little tale of

anomalies and unlimited possibilities. May it stir the musings of your mind and the quickening of your heart. As we begin to understand our own limitations as finite creatures in a vast universe of infinite complexity and intricacy, perhaps we can be released from our prejudices—whether scientific, philosophical, or religious—and open our minds to discovering more of the great plan of which we are a part.

The nineteenth-century fable *Flatland,* by Edwin Abbott, showed how people of two dimensions imprisoned anyone who mentioned three-dimension realities. Likewise, this *Story of a Clam* helps us see multiple benefits of becoming open-minded.

By every discovery, do humans learn more about the infinity of divinity? By diligence, open-mindedness, and research, can we discover over one hundredfold more about the aspects of infinite divinity than any human has yet known?

A Little about Clams*

Clam: A bivalve mollusk belonging to several marine or freshwater families of the class *Pelecypoda*. They are

*Information from the *Encyclopedia Brittanica*.

mostly a shallow-water marine mollusk, represented by more than twelve thousand species, of which about five hundred live in fresh water. Most bivalves inhabit shallow waters, where they are generally protected from wave action by the surrounding bottom.

True clams have equal shells that open and close by two adductor muscles situated at opposite ends of the shell, and a powerful, muscular, burrowing foot that can dig down into the sand. They take in food-laden water through an inhalant siphon and pass it over gills that filter oxygen and food from the water. The clam has a three-chambered heart. Its nervous system consists of three pairs of ganglia with connectives. There is no defined head region, and sense organs are concentrated in the mantle tissue.

Mollusk's eyes show the widest variation of all the sensory organs. In the bivalves, the eyes are usually situated on the edges of the mantle and at the base of the gills. Shallow water or burrowing species, such as *file shells* and *dog cockles*, have simple, light-sensitive eyes; deep water species do not have eyes.

The eastern surf clam, *Spisula Solidissima* (represented by our hero in the story), ranges from Maine to South

Carolina on the Eastern seaboard of the United States and may be found from the intertidal zone to a depth of about one hundred feet in coastal waters. Its smooth, tan-colored oval shell may reach a length of seven inches.

Prologue

"For now we see through a glass, darkly; but then face to face;
now I know in part; but then I shall know even as also
I am known." —1 Corinthians 13:12

I AM KNOWN AS COLUMBUS CLAM. Mine is a story that must be told, so I have set down my experiences, as I recall them, in this small manuscript. Throughout a most amazing, intense, and enlightening journey over a relatively short period of time, my expanding consciousness has come to recognize many great truths. Perhaps the most significant among them is the profound reality that we are not alone, that there may be intelligent beings around us that we do not yet comprehend. Another great truth is that aspects of the Divine Creator can be recognized within

9

each of us. I now understand that a vast Creative Force brought life energy into millions of species on this place called Earth, and elsewhere. Are we all—regardless of species—part of the oneness of this Great Creator? In fact, I now ask myself if *anything* can be separate from this Creative Force! Can you imagine the awesome power in this concept? Diligence, self-control, and enthusiastic research continue to propel me into further learning experiences.

I humbly admit that upon entering this Earth-life exploration, I was blessed with great beauty, charm, intelligence, and a full six-inch clamshell spread! (At least, my former clam consciousness believed this to be true.) Discernment and a pioneering attitude were not factors at my birth; I had to learn and earn these elusive things for myself. It seems that there is a special knack to discernment, and wisdom is often gleaned through experiences of painful growth. My recent journey certainly provided many opportunities to gain this important illumination.

Think not that I complain unduly, for now that I have become more enlightened, I can tell you that only a fool carps at the gifts of the Spirit! I count my sufferings as a light load when I reflect upon the increasing knowledge and many blessings I acquired with every step of this journey. I now realize that when I began, I knew as little about the Creator as I did about the great ocean in which I live and about the rich life that flourishes here.

The pain, anger, and fear of my former way of life have been borne away like foam on this vast ocean that buoyed and carried me along with it. I became an integral part of that great water. Even when my adventures seemed to drive me to the brink of insanity and when, in my lack of understanding, I raged against the Creator, I learned to recognize and love the Great Laws. The bottom-line question seems to be: "How can each of us learn to be helpers in the Great Creator's purposes?"

Now is the time of a new millennium on this planet. Many strange stories are being whispered among the population. How often a member of the community says, "Times are changing, Columbus! Times are changing."

This is true. Yet, I feel peaceful. Change doesn't scare me quite as much any more. As the present is heir to the past, so will the future be the child of the present. We can face our future and hope for a stroke of luck, or we can make conscious and constructive efforts to build our future. We can work today with a positive and exploratory attitude and diligently pursue comprehension of an ever-larger, greater Creator.

A wonderment and an expectancy are now in the air in our community. The spiritual discovery spiral is accelerating as it should. Perhaps our "coming of age" may be the major development of the twenty-first century, and through advanced thinking and intensified research by individuals such as you and me, more of us may use the tremendous abilities, now latent, that we have.

The astounding truths that I learned through my wondrous meeting with *The Keys of Opportunity* can be uplifting for me and for all of God's creatures. There are things you may learn, so you are invited to listen as I tell my tale.

—*Columbus Clam*

The Stirring 1

I AM ABOUT TO APPEAR quite inconsistent. In the telling of this story, I shall pass over many mundane details that would explain the nature of my physical existence. It is more important to relate the pertinence of the core of the Experience that changed my entire outlook than to dwell discursively on the elements of my daily life. Certainly, in the process of this journey, I experienced criticisms and rejections from residents of my former village. At times, I felt like an outcast. However, from my present perspective of life, it has become easier to comprehend why some of the "old ones" of the village were upset by what they considered "outrageous behavior." To the elders, my emerging "wild" ideas may have seemed to oppose the concepts and philosophies expressed in the sacred *Book of Clams*.

Let it suffice to say that in the beginning days of my spiritual journey, these criticisms and rejections were additional discomforts in what was becoming a painful, difficult learning situation. Yet, I could only commit myself to searching the truths that were slowly revealing themselves to me, whose cause would surely be declared in the end.

By nature, I was a focused creature whose world unfolded in a simple, uneventful manner. Though modesty prevents me from claiming more than my due, I must say that my contributions to the mollusk community had been considerable. Daily, I adhered to the tenets of the mollusks' *Book of Clams*. The wisdom found there is quite powerful: "You are the center of your world." "You are in control of your life." Effectively relating to these teachings can assist in one's success or failure, and I was a dedicated student.

Yes, I was the head of my household, and I liked it that way. All of my needs were accommodated; the universe provided appropriate support. Other than the gentle movement of the water and the subtle changing from warm light to cool darkness, the days blended in a familiar repetition.

On one particular morning, however, the surrounding waters were restless, and it took concentrated effort to keep my foot burrowed in the sand. The balance organs in my foot did not seem to be working properly. Greater effort was required to maintain stability. And those murmuring noises invading my space! It was a disturbing cacophony of sound. Now, let me tell you, I am a tolerant individual, but I did not appreciate disturbances in my domain!

The disturbances began when the geoducks, quahogs, littlenecks, and cherrystones moved into this community. I speak their names so blithely now, but what a shock it was then to learn that my fellow clams and I were not the only ones who were living in this small community! Although I had been aware of shadowy movements in the waters around me and of sometimes bumping into hard edges, and although I tried not to be narrow-minded, it had definitely required some adjustment in my thinking before I was able to accept these interlopers.

The murmuring grew louder. I thought it might be a good idea to find out what was going on.

Bump.

"Hey, watch out!"

A glimmer of communication seeped into my sluggish thoughts.

"Oops, sorry."

The erratic wave movement again tugged at my foot. Sand was slipping away, and I felt myself tumbling across the ocean bottom. I extended my foot, clutching at the sand. There! I was anchored again. Whew!

"Are you going?" A whisper floated through my mind.

"What?"

"Are you going?"

"Going where?"

"Haven't you heard the story rampaging through the Kingdom of Poseidon?"

"What story?" I was confused. The Kingdom of Poseidon? What was *that*? What had happened to *my* kingdom? Who was this interfering individual? "Who are you?"

"My name is Orca. A most marvelous treasure has been discovered near the Coral Reef. Sea folks are traveling there from vast distances in the Great Ocean to see what it's all about."

Treasure? Sea folks? Coral Reef? Orca? My mind was spinning. What nonsense was this? I had not conducted this much conversation with a stranger for quite some time. It was unusual. It was very strange!

"Surely you cannot be ignorant of this great news!" the voice continued.

Ignorant? Me? Of all the audacious statements! Some time elapsed before I could reply. I had been swept away by emotion, as I often am when confronting an incident alien to my existence. This was certainly an upsetting situation.

Rousing myself from deep reverie, I became aware the stranger was still present.

"We can travel to the Coral Reef together," Orca prompted.

A shiver ran through me and an indescribable fear seized my muddled thoughts. Important aspects of my belief system were being shaken to the core. What was happening? Again, I felt the movement of the water pull me from my anchor place in the sand. With foot flailing, I fought for stability. The waters became murky, and thick darkness descended to the bottom of the Great Ocean. I felt as if I were floating in a great abyss. I was myself and I was not myself—simultaneously. Nothing in my life's experiences compared with what was happening at that moment. Another tentacle of fear coiled around me. This disturbing situation was absolutely not acceptable!

When I could find voice, I shrieked aloud in sheer frustration and terror. At the same moment, a piercing shaft of light tore through my soul. It brought a sickening sensation of sight that was not the same as seeing visibly. (You probably are aware that mollusks' eyes show the widest variation of all the clam's sensory organs.) "I must be going mad," I wailed.

"No, you're not," a gentle voice answered. "There is more to life than you presently experience."

"What?" This voice was different from Orca's. "Have I perished and gone to the depths of Poseidon's Hades?"

"No, my friend. You are experiencing the beginning of new awareness. Breathe in deeply. You're in such a state of agitation! No harm is going to come to you. Let yourself become calm. Only open minds make discoveries."

A soothing wave of warmth flowed across my body. The light softened until it appeared as a gentle glow, permeating the waters. The fear tentacles slowly began to release their hold. I may say without egotism that when I make up my mind to do something, I do it quickly and correctly. I began to relax.

18

In an unexplainable way, I knew I was in no danger.

Friend? Was that the word spoken? What an unusual feeling that word brought to my consciousness. Consciousness? What is *that*, and where did it come from? A cold shiver slid through my shells.

"Relax, Columbus. This may be the time for a look at a broader framework for life's meaning than the one presented in the *Book of Clams*."

"The *Book of Clams*! You know about *that* great work? Who are *you*?"

"I am a part of you—an aspect of your being that it is time for you to be aware of. I am also a part of that which is called 'Creation.' And a part of what is called the 'Great Creator.' These ideas may seem strange to you at the moment, but bear with me. When research prompts a movement toward greater growth, we are often faced with the limitation of our own minds. The search for greater reality is the impetus behind the excitement moving throughout the Great Ocean."

"You know about the Coral Reef?"

"Yes. And I am here to assist you through the change in which your physical reality is emerging."

"What happened to Orca?"

"He continued on his journey to the Coral Reef."

Definitely there were points to ponder! I was in a somewhat anomalous position. While not entirely unhappy with this position, especially in its more careful and nuanced handling, I certainly desired to know *what was taking place*!

"Columbus, will you . . . ?"

"Oh, do be quiet and allow me to think!"

The *Book of Clams* did say something along the lines of "the more we learn, the more there is to know."

Silence.

It was time to proceed to facts. An unnamed energy stirred the waters of the Great Ocean. The mollusk community was not unique. Sea folk (whoever they were) were traveling to the Coral Reef (wherever that was). Rumors were circulating about something called *The Keys of Opportunity*. Strange voices were communicating with me. Such assertions could be easily made, but not easily proved. Fascinating speculation! What an imagination! What was the possible counter to this conjecture?

"I can show you truth."

There it was again. Just when I thought a certain kind of normality had been restored to my world. Restraining my impatience, I asked, "Who did you say you were?"

"I didn't. However, you may call me Agape."

"Agape? What does that mean? Where are you from? Why me?"

"*Agape* means 'pure unlimited love,' Columbus. This may be a new concept for you, but you are ready for the next step in your evolution. I am here to assist you as the still, small voice of the Great Creator."

"I don't know about this . . ."

"Columbus, you have nothing to lose and everything to gain through our association. You are a product of millenniums of evolutionary steps. There is an avenue where creative interaction may take place, but in which each field may retain its own appropriate foundation. Would you hold up progress until you have objective proof?"

"I don't know what you're talking about."

"Of course you don't. This is all new to your consciousness. But you are like the 'field white unto the harvest.' You are ready to take this journey; otherwise, you would not be hearing my voice and responding—albeit rather hesitantly."

"I feel so tired. And heavy. And sleepy. This situation is more than I can absorb."

"It's all right, Columbus. Let your thoughts rest. The world is a far stranger and more baffling place than you realize. It is full of creative surprises, and you are beginning to sense something imaginative, purposeful, and powerful taking place. Relax, Columbus. Feel the warmth of the light enveloping you. Only open minds make discoveries."

Strange as it sounds, I could feel a warm, soft glow all around me like a comforting presence. Even the restless waters seemed momentarily calmed. My defiance began to evaporate like the smile of a humpback whale. There were definitely real issues with which to deal, but something deep inside was urging me to commit myself to this truth that Agape mentioned. If this new information was indeed truth, it would prevail in the end anyway.

I clamped my shells together tightly and retreated.

Stranger in the Midst 2

"COLUMBUS, WAKE UP." The voice was soft, yet penetrating.

I stirred and began to move my body in the sand. The warm waters flowing around my shell felt cleansing and refreshing. After I had enjoyed this movement at great length, I responded, "What?"

"Wake up. There is much to be accomplished today."

I sighed, indignant at being disturbed, and attempted to bring myself into some semblance of awareness.

"Columbus."

There it was again. The persistent voice that had shaken the foundation of my world yesterday was continuing into the new day. "Go away. Leave me alone. You're not supposed to be here. You're not even *real*."

"Columbus, what are you?"

Persistent and infuriating creature!

"I am a clam. And I would be a much more peaceful clam if you would simply disappear from my mind and leave me alone."

"Oh, is that all?"

"What do you mean, 'Is that all?' Being a clam has suited me just fine all of my life." This Agape Clam, or whatever the creature was called, was as irritating as a misplaced grain of sand. "A clam is a highly respectable creation. The ultimate. The best. Top of the line, in fact!"

"Could it be that what you presently perceive is only a tiny, temporary manifestation of reality?"

What a nuisance! "My perception is true. My world is *the* world and clams are the dominant life form."

"Yes, Columbus, I understand where you're coming from. How could you think otherwise when all of your perspectives have been focused in a particular arena throughout a short lifetime."

"Just what are you getting at?" By now I was fully awake and ready to give this intruder a bit of clam advice!

"Columbus, let's take a look at something familiar."

"Like what?"

"Your shell, for example."

"Why?"

"So you can glean more understanding of what you are and, perhaps, why you were created."

Silence. No one was going to push me into anything. Yet, there was something titillating about this Agape being. I *was* somewhat curious.

"Look at the inside of your shell, Columbus."

"Now that's a dumb statement! How can I look at the inside of myself?"

"Feel your shell around you. Give intent to see inside your house."

"Give intent? What's that?"

"Let your desire to learn what you are like become uppermost in your thoughts."

"Hm-m-m."

"How did your shell begin?"

Silence. I didn't have a clue, but I wasn't telling *him* that!

"It began as a calciferous liquid that was secreted by your soft mantle tissue and then hardened."

Made absolutely no sense to me. However, he seemed to enjoy hearing himself talk, so I thought I'd just keep quiet.

"Columbus?"

"Yes?"

"Now, imagine that you can magnify or turn up or increase what you are able to see."

By the great *Book of Clams*! Patience was not one of my strengths, but I was intrigued by this mystery. Something was happening. It appeared that I *could* become more aware of my house. I could vaguely "see" the innermost layer of nacre, or mother-of-pearl, very close by.

"That's correct, Columbus. Now you're getting it. Keep focusing on your shell. Feel your awareness going beyond the nacre layer, to the central layer, which is made of prismatic calcium carbonate crystals."

I still didn't comprehend what he was talking about, but it *did* seem as if something glistened at a deeper level. Nonetheless, I was working hard at reserving judgment about the whole situation.

"Now, Columbus, intend your awareness to move a little deeper and notice the outer, organic layer of your home called the periostracium."

I was lost. I really didn't understand what all of this meant. What was the purpose of this strange happening? How was it going to make my life better?

"Columbus, if you could look deeply enough to turn up the magnification to a much greater level, you could discern individual cells in the different layers of your shell structure. And each cell would loom as large and complex as a city with its boundaries delineated by the cell walls. If you increased the magnification even further, you could see within the cell an entire neighborhood of complex apparatus devoted to the respiratory, sanitary, and energy-producing functions that maintain each cell of your body."

Whew! I was getting the feeling that much more lay behind this fascinating world of particles and forces than I understood. I didn't know whether I liked the way this discussion—or rather, *lecture* from this Agape Clam—was going.

"Yes, this is all new to you, Columbus. However, let me assure you that at the bottom of it all is a wondrously complex and simple idea. Some things are not for us to understand immediately; we must seek and welcome discoveries. And I believe that when you discover the composition of that idea, it will be so compelling, so inevitable, that we will agree with each other, 'Oh, how magnificent! How could it be otherwise?' A willingness to learn and a commitment to search for and discover truth principles can be foundation stones to greater knowledge."

A wondrously complex and simple idea. Now that was a dichotomy if I ever heard one. I supposed that theoretically this truth, if such it was, was unquestionable. But I'm a practical clam and refrain from total acceptance of any new inclinations without first looking for the practical drawbacks. I wondered what the weak point in this theory was, and again, how would this information improve my life and enhance my productivity?

"Columbus, information alone is powerless to improve your life unless you put it to work."

"What do you mean, 'put it to work'?"

"Well, it's like this. Do you know what a stairway is?"

"Stairway?"

"All right, let's put the analogy in your vernacular. Sometimes when you travel along the bottom of the sea floor, you may come to a level that is higher than your present position. How do you navigate up to that next level?"

"That's simple. I feel the wave movement of the water around me. I allow my body to move in harmony with it, and when a particularly strong flow comes along, I use

28

my foot and jump. The wave movement and my effort together lift me to the higher level of the sea floor."

"Excellent! The levels of the sea floor can be like an ascending stairway. Each step that you take upward can bring you into greater awareness. The first step may seem almost nonexistent—a faint glimmer in consciousness. Remember how you were aware of activity in the Great Ocean around you before your meeting with Orca? Things seemed dark and unfocused."

There was truth in the statement. I remained silent.

"The next step may bring you some kind of awareness that there is more to the universe than your small and seemingly safe and secure world. This is where we are now."

Yeah. Right.

"With another step, you may encounter a blinding light that will blast everything you've ever believed to utter chaos. However, it is this light—the Light of Universal Intelligence—that will help you understand that you are so much more than one small clam in the Great Ocean. You may begin to feel a powerful energy that affirms you are part of something really big. You are part of a majestic, wondrous, *whole*.

"If you are persistent in your desire to expand your awareness, the next several steps you take may be clouded in mystery as you learn more about this wondrous whole and contemplate its meaning and your role in its unfolding. At this particular time in your evolution, you may vacillate between emotional highs and lows as your consciousness moves through a very rapid period of expansion. This process can be quite unsettling, but it can lead to the realization of why you were created."

"Created?"

"Yes, Columbus. Created. Your own *Book of Clams* brings you a certain awareness of the Great Creator. You have survived in your world by applying the principles in this book to your daily life. This is well and good. You have accomplished much—especially as you became more aware of others in your community. Although you fought against this new knowledge, that which is true reveals itself eventually.

"You are strong, Columbus Clam. Although you may not consciously know it at this time, your soul—the essence of your reality—is ready to grow. And I am here to help you take the next steps."

"I don't know what to say to all of this."

"It isn't necessary to say anything, Columbus. You have had much information heaped upon your head. Come away for a while in thoughtful contemplation, and ponder the things I have presented to you. I'll be close by if you have questions or simply want to talk. I'm as close as your thoughts."

"I don't doubt that. It's impossible to get away from you!"

"Oh, Columbus! We've only just begun. The universe has extra, hidden dimensions that may seem to play no real role in your world, but everything is intricately interwoven, and your clam-centered ideas about being all there is have already been shattered. You will never be the same again.

"There are a lot of energies we haven't touched upon. More will unfold in a divine pattern of progression of intelligence and love as we continue our communication."

I couldn't handle any more information at that point. It was fast becoming apparent that my "doesn't affect me" attitude was no longer workable. Things seemed to be getting more chaotic and more and more complicated. What was a clam to do?

Begin with a Single Point 3

PERHAPS, DEAR READER, you may be beginning to perceive the tremendous upheavals that took place in my life at the start of this adventure. Such a life I had then! In retrospect, I can see that during the time my vision was limited to a single focus (me), living was inexpressibly dreary. Although, to be truthful, my consciousness then was too vague to realize it. However, with the advent of Agape's emergence into my consciousness—but wait! I don't want to get ahead of my story.

After several days of reflecting on the things Agape had spoken of, I reached a decision. I had to determine where this new information would lead. I recalled reading somewhere in the *Book of Clams* that it is deeply meaningful to accept the things to which life connects you and to be agreeable to the clams with whom fate brings you together, that every clam in your life has a reason for being there. The great book of wisdom also emphasizes the importance of being courteous to other clams but intimate with few, and of letting those few be well tried before you give them your full confidence. It also affirms that a good relationship with another clam is a plant of slow growth—like good sea coral—and needs to undergo and withstand the shock of adversity before it is entitled to be called wisdom.

Yes, I was ready to continue my journey of exploration. Some unknown factor assured me that no matter what difficulties I might go through, the situation could be changed for the better. There would be a solution and a way, but it would be important for me to define the source of the problem and move toward a successful solution. For my personal growth to begin, I would have to recognize the undesirable habits that I had allowed to become entrenched in my life and acknowledge their influence on my actions.

It is amazing how many seemingly unconnected events bring us to the next phase of growth. We may not notice the little "incidences" in the moment when they are happening. But they produce their effect. A tiny wisp of a thought can inspire still more thoughts, eventually setting into motion a remarkable new chain of possibilities.

On this particular morning, everything around me reflected disturbance. The wave movement was especially turbulent, and in my slowly increasing awareness of things outside myself, the cacophony around me became almost unbearable. The entire clam community seemed to be rampaging over the sea floor and landing in a disheveled heap. Dark shadows filtering through the faint ripples of light bespoke giant creatures swimming overhead. Although I remained somewhat apart from the clam community, I was aware of the discomfort and disturbance of the clan.

It is difficult to describe what happened next. One moment I was a fairly detached observer of an upsetting situation, and the next moment I was caught up in a thrashing, splashing, swirling tsunami. I was caught in the grips of a powerful energy that was moving me to . . . Poseidon knows where!

"Agape! Where are you? Help!"

No response.

I called again, "Agape, where are you when I need you? Help!"

Still no response.

At that moment, everything screeched to a halt, and my awareness slammed into the most unusual imagery. In fact, my mind still swims when I recall the details of what happened next. At first, it was difficult to determine just what was taking place, for I was extremely disoriented. A similar feeling had persisted since my first "meeting" with Agape and his revelations, but this was different. Beyond feeling disoriented, I also felt the presence of a compelling and foreign energy.

Suddenly, a strong impulse, almost like a voice, told me to remain perfectly still. A little tremor of fear swirled along my shell rim, and my shock was so powerful that I did what I was told.

I became aware of an unbelievable spectacle. I was lying on the sea floor alongside an enormous room. I later learned that this was a large and deep lagoon. As my sensors scanned the area, I heard a babble of every conceivable squeal, squeak, snort, hum, and rumble, identified with names like whales, dolphins, stingrays, and eels—to list just a few. Of course none of them were

36

comprehensible to my confused mind. These animate beings were everywhere! I was bumped and jostled as everyone swam around in what appeared to be mass confusion. One of the creatures came down hard on my shell, pressing me into the sand. I struggled to lift myself on my foot.

I collapsed. I was filled with fear. What was happening? Who were these creatures? Why was I there? None of this made any sense. Then *It* arrived.

Slowly, ever so gently, a faint rhythm pulsed through the waters. The pulsing increased in intensity until it was vibrating inside my shell. Realizing that everything was getting blurry, I tried to look around. There! At the other end of the lagoon, something very large was materializing! It became clearer and clearer until I beheld a most unusual individual. It appeared to be standing on fins that gently swept the water, and fin-like flappers, moving in an oar-like fashion, held the creature in position.

The large body of the creature, a classic example of expert streamlining, glistened sleek and smooth in the water. Above the upper jaw was a large mass that looked like a bulging forehead. I could see a bottle-shaped snout and sharp, conical teeth as the beast appeared to be emitting some sort of sound. His compelling appearance represented the very prime of life, and any idea of age as connected with him would have been absurd.

"It's the Dolphin Prince!" someone nearby whispered.

A hush immediately settled over the inhabitants of the lagoon. Next I heard a series of short, pulse-type sounds produced in rapid succession. I later learned such sounds are used as a form of sonar called echolocation.

"Something pretty major must be happening."

"I wonder why he's here."

"Sh-h-h, I want to hear what he has to say."

At that moment, the only audible sound in the lagoon was the movement of the water, back and forth, as the tide surged and ebbed.

The Dolphin Prince seemed to expand in stature as he emitted a high-pitched whistle to ensure everyone's attention. I dug my foot more securely into the sand and waited. Something akin to excitement tingled in my being.

"Greetings to each of you, my fellow sea folk," the Dolphin Prince saluted everyone.

A soft murmur and faint stirring of acknowledgment circulated among everyone gathered. Energy flowed all through the lagoon. The environment immediately became tranquil and my mind responded. I could feel myself getting into a listening and reflective state. I had never experienced such a mood of restfulness combined with excited anticipation. Energy continued to move around and within me. The spaces and boundaries that had existed between me and the others present began to melt. I couldn't call this a physical sensation, but something more whole, complete, and unified.

Whole! Agape had said something about a "whole." I wondered if this strange energy was what he meant. Of course, I can provide this description now but at the time of the event, I was a muddled mess!

The lagoon glowed with a soft, diffused light, as though the sun had turned up its radiance several degrees to pour down through the waters.

The Dolphin Prince spoke. "Each of you is present for this meeting, drawn here by right of consciousness."

Right of consciousness? I made a mental note to ask Agape about that expression the next time he made himself known.

"Many of you have heard the rumor that a wonderful treasure has been found, and some of you are traveling to the great Coral Reef to learn more about it. At this moment in history, our planet and its inhabitants stand at the portal of extraordinary change, and *The Keys of Opportunity* can represent a threshold for our greater awakening."

Planet? What was that? *Inhabitants.* That one I was beginning to understand.

"The awakening I speak of is a deeper understanding of what and who you are, and why. It begins with a single point: the willingness to accept your place in the flow of evolution and become responsible for yourself and your actions. The approaching awakening brings you an opportunity to participate, to a larger degree, in the power of the Great Creator. As you reach a greater understanding of the enormity of what is happening, you may experience thoughts and feelings totally foreign to your ego. When this occurs, it becomes important to release the illusion that you are in any way separate from the rest of life and to focus on the Divine drama that is unfolding. Truly, this is a time of great transformation for the many species living in the Great Ocean."

The Dolphin Prince continued his communication, but all thought was gone from my mind at that moment.

I felt like a tangled mass of protoplasm searing on a hot sand beach somewhere. A statement from the *Book of Clams* streaked through my consciousness: *He who centers his focus on the Great Creator can be strong in heart and peaceful.* Yeah! Right! It isn't easy!

As if he knew my innermost turmoil, the Dolphin Prince continued his remarks. "Try to resist the urge to drift away from what is happening. You are simply reacting to your fear of the unknown. In this instance, fear is an attempt to block your vision of yourself, to fail to perceive yourself as you truly are. Many have convinced themselves that they are weak and open to attack. Quite the opposite is true. The Great Creator has formed every one of you in the image of Divine life. You are one with that life. What was created whole cannot be divided, but it can be falsely perceived. This is primarily the role of fear, to perceive perfection as imperfect, and to see what is true as false. This is called illusion, and you'll learn more about it later.

"You already know from your recent experiences that the Great Ocean is changing, evolving. Past, present, and future have real meaning. The past of itself can have no power over us except that which we allow. We can learn much from the past. Both our mistakes and our accomplishments provide fertile soil for advancement. It has taken untold time to get where we presently are, and there is no known limit to where or how much further we can go. The present is *now*. Things are happening. Look at the amazing experiences that occur in daily life. The world is a far stranger and more baffling place than we had thought—full of creative surprise—even to the point of generating sentient beings such as ourselves. It isn't difficult to sense something vastly more imaginative, purposeful, and powerful taking place."

Well! That statement certainly sounded familiar!

"*Transformation* is one name for the conditions now occurring in the Great Ocean. The agency of this transformation has many names and facets, and its exquisite products suggest that something quite beyond random forces is involved.

"What is important for you to know at this time is that you can become more intelligent about your world. Instinct may say this is a risk for some of you. It is! The risk is to dare to learn new things and put your new knowledge to work in your life."

Sounded like Agape again.

"Remember this one thing. What you give your attention and belief to becomes your experience. So, focus your attention on the way you would like to see yourself, and the kind of world in which you want to live. If you look at life from one point of view, everything may seem unstable. This feeling of instability is what many of you are presently experiencing. But look at the universe another way, and everything is alive and growing! Everything is in joyous motion. New combinations and even species appear. New wisdom touches your soul. New opportunities abound. Will you welcome the adventure?"

The Dolphin Prince paused and looked around the lagoon at those assembled. His presence and words were riveting. I was stunned—the only word for my reaction to the overwhelming inundation of information. As I glanced around, I could tell I was not alone in my incredulity. Others were staring at the Dolphin Prince with blank, shocked looks.

The Dolphin Prince waved a flipper. "One more thing. I am traveling to the great Coral Reef. I hope you will join me in my journey." He turned and headed toward the entrance of the lagoon.

The lagoon again filled with sound as those around me stirred from their stupor and murmured among themselves. I couldn't move. The entire situation was frightening and unbelievable.

As the Dolphin Prince passed nearby, I thought I heard him say, "You were brought here because you are capable of making the shift to a higher level of consciousness. Try to relax and be patient. Everything is in order."

Once again, disorientation swept over me. My inner vision and consciousness began to fade. The present and the future dimmed. At that moment, some force of energy from the depths of my being emerged from its habitat and yelled, "Don't you dare give in to these unsettling emotions. Stand strong and *be* what you can be!"

Expanding World 4

"THE SECURITY YOU DESIRE so much in your life and what you are seeking in your small community is a false security. It depends on conditions that will ever change and on the stability of the perspectives you develop to manage those changing conditions, although, from the larger picture, these changes may seem minute. Columbus Clam, the reality you presently have in life is change!"

I could feel my consciousness awakening slowly.

"Agape?"

"Yes, Columbus. I am present in your thoughts."

"Where have you been? Why can't I see you?"

"I have always been one with you. You cannot see me because I am spirit energy, without visible form and yet as real as the Great Ocean and your clamshell. You are consciously aware of my presence, which can be one form of 'seeing the unseen'."

"I don't perceive the connection."

"Allow yourself the gift of exploration, Columbus. It can propel you into wondrous worlds that you cannot presently comprehend. I would like to encourage the idea of an interactive, expanding relationship between you and me and realms, or levels, of awareness."

"Am I ready for that?"

"As ready as you will ever be!"

"It's too radical a change in my world!"

"Columbus, you've only touched on a tiny fragment of the awareness that can be achieved."

"I have no time to attend to the expression of opinions which, whether good or bad, are of no difference to me."

"That's the old clam consciousness speaking. That's the part of you that is extremely resistant to change and whose world has been turned upside down. Columbus, I give you this assurance. Whether you, who wander in the shadows of your own making, care to move toward the light that can lead you onward, or whether you choose to turn away from our connection altogether, the decision is completely yours. I do not, and would not, desire to compel you to journey with me. Even the Great Creator does not do that, for it is his will and law that each soul shall shape its own eternal future."

Hmmph!

"Many journey in the wilderness and know that there are ways of making the seemingly barren wilderness blossom like sea anemones. Nevertheless, despite your possible indifference, I cannot in all love pass you by without offering to share that love with you. The hour is at hand when those who inhabit the Great Ocean shall give more recognition to the activity of the Great Creator. Creativity needs intellectual cooperation between the outer, physical life and the eternal progression of the inner spirit. Evolution is one aspect of this accelerating creativity."

After that flow of commentary, I was properly subdued, as well as totally mystified.

"Columbus?"

"Yes?"

"What happened yesterday in the lagoon?"

"You know about *that* experience?"

"Of course."

"Where were *you* when all that was happening?"

"Close . . . and observing."

"It was a most upsetting experience. Evidently the Great Ocean is considerably larger than any clam has ever imagined."

"It is. And life is bringing you a grand opportunity, Columbus."

"How so?"

"It would appear, based on information from the High Council, that various realities are becoming more and more accurately described."

"What's the High Council?"

"The High Council is a large group of individuals who have committed their lives to the increasing betterment of all of life. They select many subjects for increasing scientific research and probability reasoning and discussion. Their work becomes intricate at times, but the predominant purpose of the Council is the mental, physical, spiritual, and scientific betterment of all, as complementary avenues to truth. It is possible for sentient creation to live in the radiance of the soul, regardless of the material conditions surrounding the body."

"How was what happened yesterday a 'grand opportunity'?"

48

"We're vacillating wildly in this conversation, Columbus. Let's take one thing at a time and meet on a similar plane of thought instead of wandering separately. What you experienced yesterday in the lagoon offers you and the other sea folk an opportunity for transformation—self-organization—and its exquisite products strongly suggest that something quite beyond random forces was involved. For the soul that has found itself (and yes, Columbus, the Great Creator's spark is within you), there are no more misleading lights or shadows between its own eternal life and the infinity of the Great Creator."

Agape was talking like the Dolphin Prince. Slowly brightening, slowly widening, a pale radiance like the earliest glimmer of sunlight slipped gently around me. Strains of something harmonious drifted through the waters. I later learned what I heard and felt was the music of whale song from a pod passing nearby. At the moment, it seemed enough to simply *be* in the energy of the sound and light and the presence of Agape.

"Tell me more, please."

"Columbus, the amazing process of transformation, or self-revelation, accompanies self-existence. You can never detach yourself from your own penetrating, enveloping energy, either in body or in soul. The wise one taught this when he said, 'Let your light so shine before all that they may see your good works and give glory to the Great Creator.'"

"Do you know what your 'light' is, Columbus?"

"No. The word sounds like I've heard it before, but I don't know what it means."

"'Light' is a way of stating who and what you are and can be. Light is a powerful energy, and it is produced and exhaled by your physical and mortal body. And some, those who have cultivated their inner ability of vision, may be aware of your light energy before they actually see your physical body. Your light can shimmer in pure radiance, or it can be a mere nebulous film."

"When the Dolphin Prince was so strong and power-ful while in the lagoon, was that because of his 'light'?"

"That is correct, Columbus. The Dolphin Prince is a magnificent being who has gleaned much wisdom from his vast experiences. He knows the truth of what he speaks. His father is one who sits with the High Council, and the Dolphin Prince confers with his father fre-quently. And fortunately for all, one of the Prince's greatest desires is to share what he knows with others.

50

"Agape, I feel filled to overflowing with all the information you and others are providing. I sincerely desire to assimilate the wisdom from these experiences, but I sometimes feel very small. Will this awesome comprehension of the Great Creator continue?"

"Yes. And it will expand even more rapidly. Also, Columbus, you may begin to comprehend at a faster speed. One of my purposes is to assist you in integrating your spiritual awareness into your day-to-day reality. Integration is not a static state. It is a flow that moves in an orderly progression, although presently you may feel inundated. An integrated clam, when approached with new information, will take a moment to listen to the information, to fully hear what is being presented, and to then proceed to bring into form an appropriate action. The time may arrive soon, Columbus, when you can more easily accept these ideas. Continue your search for greater truth. Finding is a result of searching, and searching for good is good for you. Be receptive to whatever comes your way, for open minds are ready to grow. Listen, and make your choices about how to use what you learn. Hopefully, a portion of what you are receiving may be of some practical value to you now. If so, I am happy to be of service."

I reflected for a while on what Agape had said. The idea of the "wilderness" came to my mind. I was vaguely aware of desolate portions of the sea floor that were barren of clam communities, according to the *Book of Clams*. All of a sudden, I felt as if I were in the middle of one of those wilderness areas. I crouched listlessly near a large sunken log, too weary to move. Apparently, I had wandered far away from the clam community; I wondered how soon and where this journey would end. The veil of mere appearances continued to lift, and I began to feel deceived by ignorance, improper balance, and certainly by an imperfect comprehension of my "clamness."

"Agape?"

"Yes, Columbus?"

"Tell me more about you. Perhaps listening to what you have to say can move my thoughts away from my own miserable situation. You said you were always near. How? Why?"

"Yes, Columbus, I am as near as your thoughts. How do I come to communicate with you? The best response I can presently give, which you will understand more fully as your comprehension expands, is that the Great Creator provides an access for each creature to understand his true position in the scale of the creative and progressive purpose. At this very time, and in this very world, there abide astounding blessings, unused powers, and precious possibilities. It may be said truthfully that the great majority of beings inhabiting this place have scarcely begun to learn how to live.

"You are not asked to accept everything that comes to you, but rather to consider other perspectives. Honor the energy that may have drawn you to sharing a different view. Your innate wisdom—and, yes, Columbus, I use that word 'wisdom' correctly—can guide you to accept truth as it resonates in your consciousness. There is no power, creature-wise or divine, that could compel you to remain in ignorance.

"There is an ever-living spirit within each of us for which there is no limited capacity and no unfavorable surroundings. The spirit helps the questing consciousness bring every feeling and sense into closer union with the Great Creator and his eternal assistant, Nature. Nature is simply the reflection of the manifesting mind of the Great Creator.

"Why am I with you? I am here through the expressive energy of my being, represented by my name. Agape.

Pure, Unlimited Love. Do you know what Unlimited Love is, Columbus?"

"No."

"I'll attempt to explain, although it is something you *are* more than something words can explain. Agape, or Unlimited Love, is a deliberate choice, one you can make at any time. It does not depend on how you feel, but on loving regardless of how you feel. The Great Creator is Unlimited Love. And that love must spring spontaneously from the Creator's spark within each one. When you give love, you live in the pure essence of the Great Creator, and the Great Creator's essence fills your being and your world. This kind of love is unconquerable and irresistible. It continues gathering power and spreading itself until it eventually transforms everyone it touches. When we give all the love we are capable of giving at any time, we find we still have even more love left. Giving love increases love, and giving more love can be a turning point for the soul. Unlimited Love can wash away all conflicts. These are blessed moments when the hardships of life give way to an awakening to the presence of the Great Creator.

"It takes courage to rise above the status quo, Columbus. It requires the kind of bravery that each of us must learn in our own way. I'm here because I am a part of you and I love you."

"Agape, I cannot describe what I am presently feeling. I feel complete, whatever that means, as if I am about to fulfill some role I have been preparing for throughout my entire life, but didn't realize it. I don't understand at all, except that for the first time since these experiences began, I feel warm and happy."

"That's very good, Columbus. You are feeling the light energy of my love for you. Relax and enjoy its soothing sensation. Allow yourself to experience the feeling of my love for you. Allowing and permitting are elements of receptivity and awareness. Begin to explore these areas within yourself. The evolution of this new pattern will happen in its own time. Be thankful to yourself for your growth, for the challenges you have met, and for those yet to come. Remember, you are beloved of the Great Creator."

Agape's words faded away as I felt myself slip into the warm embrace of the energy around me. The wilderness disappeared. As I relaxed into the wonderful sphere of Agape's love, a strange, penetrating but gentle tone went straight to the center of my clam consciousness. I knew the time would come when I would contemplate deeply the things of which Agape had spoken. I felt there was much more to be known, and I loved to explore. I deeply longed to be shown the latitudes and longitudes of truth—if such invisible boundaries even exist. A gentle inner awareness whispered that something new and beautiful awaited me as I pressed on in my voyage of discovery. The last thing I remember Agape saying are these caressing words: "Love makes all things beautiful, Columbus, and one who is conscious of being loved grows lovely, as a rose that is conscious of the sun grows elegant in form and vibrant in color. Sleep, my Friend."

"A rose? I must ask Agape to explain 'a rose'."

All was quiet. All was well. For the moment.

Crossroads 5

HAT WAS TO BECOME a long and sultry day dawned in the world of the Great Ocean. Even so early in the morning, a heavy heat sank into the troubled waters. A lingering darkness hung in the lower depths of Poseidon's kingdom, although a thin line of light tried valiantly to pierce the ocean depths. It was the merest taper-flame, reflecting the glowing eastern sky, and it marked the passage of time for Columbus Clam.

When the light penetrated the waters, I knew it was day. When it vanished, I knew night had arrived. Otherwise, the passage of minutes and hours were indistinguishable. My existence had merged into one long protracted phase of dull suffering, unexplainable excitement, and discussions with Agape. These alternations left me stupefied.

At the moment, I had no particular consciousness of anything except that needlepoint of light that fell obliquely upon me. For quite some time the energy of change moved everywhere and was apparently affecting all the sea creatures. Writhing back under the sunken log as far as I could, I was seized with unrest. I made querulous complaint of the situation as a whole and dug my foot deeper into the soft sand. I was alone—yet not altogether alone, for I could hear and feel the movement of other sea creatures in the surrounding waters.

"Columbus."

I turned with a swift movement that almost pulled my foot from the soft sand. "What now? And where have you been? I've worked myself into a considerable state of upset over the things you've been telling me and the critical comments about my behavior by some members of the clam community!"

"It is time for an important discussion, Columbus. There is much additional information for you to become more aware of and little time to learn it."

I uttered no comment of either surprise or interest;

I was still trying to gather my thoughts.

"Columbus, you have your old life as a clam, and there is a huge wall between you and your progression on the other side of that wall. The wall is called 'change.' You are realizing within yourself that you are going to have to modify your life in order to go through that change. To accelerate discovery of new information requires diligence and enthusiasm. Progress often stalls because individuals close their minds, egotistically believing that they already know the total truth. The Great Creator's love and intelligent, creative mind form a ladder that can assist you in getting over the wall of ignorance. You can absolutely depend on the Great Creator for assistance in every situation because the Great Creator loves you.

"Often when major changes come upon us, we become paralyzed with fear. We may go into our protective shells and not want to move. But one of the best ways to have a clean, clear mind is to change it now and then in a positive manner. To have a new view and new opinion of your own individual life may seem risky; however, you can't fall back into the old pattern, because time marches on. Even if you chose not to continue in your journey of progression, you could never go back to your old way of life because the 'real' you now lives in a different state of awareness. Life is not something that is here today and gone tomorrow. Life is continuous. Life is eternal. And, yes, the Great Creator will always allow you the time you need to grow. You are learning astounding things, Columbus. You are in the school of life. Now is the time of choice. What is your decision, Columbus?"

"Why is this happening to me? Why couldn't things stay the way they were?"

"Again, Columbus, your time of growth has arrived. You are ready to take the next step. If you reflect back to our early communication, can you remember what you were like? Do you remember the egotistical, self-centered clam that believed he was the Great Creator's ultimate work? Can you recall the dark, shadowy substance of your consciousness before you felt the light of awakening?"

I tried to remember—and couldn't. That former time seemed to me like a vague and distant dream. I made no answer.

"Columbus, when individuals go through change, several reactions are natural. I want to share those with you so you may more clearly understand what is happening.

60

"First, at the moment you may be feeling awkward and uncomfortable. You may also feel somewhat self-conscious and want to hide. How do you cope with these feelings? One way is to make it all right to be where you are for the moment. Even though your clam shells may be clattering, remind yourself that the presence of the Great Creator is everywhere and that you are safe.

"Realize that it is normal sometimes to feel alone when going through a change."

He was certainly correct on that point! I reflected for a moment on the attitudes of some of my former associates. I could have called one fellow "Fearful Clam" because he was so filled with fear of everything that he was hardly aware of anything outside his clam shells. Another was so rigid in his perceptions that any new idea would have bounced off his shells. Yes, I could identify with feeling alone.

"This is all right. How do you take charge of this feeling of aloneness? One way to do it is: don't isolate yourself. Remember, others of the sea folk are also experiencing different levels of readiness for change. And there are others who desire to research this new information and the ensuing circumstances. Reach out to them, and respond when they reach out to you. In this manner, you can work together with others and give and receive encouragement. Much joy comes from a giving attitude. In humility (and you'll soon learn more about this great character trait), we can learn from each other. Humility helps us become more receptive to others, and it can open wondrous doors to the realms of the spirit."

"I want to talk with you more about these 'others'."

"We will discuss this shortly, Columbus. I first wish to explain a couple of other possible reactions. You may, at some point along the way, feel you don't have enough resources or abilities to meet these changes. Let me assure you that you are created with every ability and resource necessary for your growth. The Great Creator made you complete in your uniqueness. And sometimes progress comes after a careful assessment of your present position. You are like an ocean wave that is a tiny, temporary manifestation of the Great Ocean of which the wave is a part. This analogy describes our relationship to the Great Creator.

"Finally, and this is important, maintain your focus for growth. Allow your concentration to serve as a tension for progress. Stretch yourself to go in a new way—in the direction of positive change. Try always to surpass yourself. You can alter the old patterns of thinking and adjust to changing circumstances.

"Now, Columbus, what is your question about the 'others'?"

"Well, I have certainly learned that there are other sea folk because I have met some of them. The clam community does not represent the totality of the Great Creator's work. Are there intelligent creatures surrounding us that we do not yet comprehend?"

"Oh, Columbus, the vastness of the Creator's work is truly mind-boggling. Varieties of creatures already exist right here in this vicinity. And each one is connected with the creative force that is present in all beings. You've experienced such a tiny portion of the Great Ocean that this idea may require some of that 'stretching' I mentioned earlier. If you desire progress, remain open-minded. Seek the new adventures, for those who do not seek are not likely to find. One of the guidelines for progress is to work diligently in the present, with your focus trained on the future."

I thought about this idea. Something deep within affirmed that an important truth was being given to me.

"Agape, is the Dolphin Prince a highly progressed being?"

"He is one who has allowed his mind to be receptive to many great truths that have been presented to him. Do you remember how you felt when the Dolphin Prince was speaking in the lagoon?"

"Yes. But I can't really describe what it was like."

"Columbus, each being has a personal concept of the Great Creator. It is important to listen carefully, thoughtfully, and gratefully to everyone's concept of the Great Creator and his purposes for his creation. Much wisdom can come to you through a listening attitude. By studying the behavior of those with whom you come in contact, it would soon be apparent to you that the happiest and most productive among them are the ones who rejoice in the well-being and good fortune of others. These are the ones who are willing to offer assistance whenever it is needed."

"Why are these things important for me to know, Agape? And how can I know that the Great Creator lives in me and I am really contained in this tremendous creative energy?"

"I'll respond to your second question first, Columbus.

Your present concept of the Great Creator is too small. This is understandable, for you are in the midst of a major shift in your consciousness into greater awareness. Your concept of the Great Creator has been finite rather than infinite. Even your precious *Book of Clams*, meaningful as it may be, may offer an incomplete awareness of the Great Truth. You see, Columbus, truth is so vast that no one particular perception of truth can present its complete essence. Usually a progressive, far-reaching thinker is one who breaks out of a traditional mold to bring new ideas of the creative process and our place in it. We must somehow encourage our gifted individuals to dedicate their time and talents to the study of this ongoing work of creation. Learning is a lifetime activity of vast importance. We continually need new breakthroughs for our increasing understanding of the Great Creator. And it seems that overall awareness and progress is speeding up!

"How can you know the Great Creator lives within you, Columbus? Look around you. Review the events of the past few weeks. Evaluate where you are in your awareness now as compared with where you were when we first began communication. What are your feelings?

What prompted your awakening? And what has continued to elicit your interest in this awakening? You may find answers to these questions as you continue to grow. As you seek and find, Columbus, there may be additional seeking and finding. Along the path of this journey will come those moments of pure inspiration when you will *know* the touch of the Creator's life within you. When this occurs, there is no further doubt of your connection with the Great Creator. It is a marvelous personal experience, and no one can tell you how your own realization will happen.

"In response to your first question, Columbus, you are on the threshold of one of the greatest adventures of your life! You are at a crossroads, and your choice of direction can forever change how you perceive yourself and your world. If you choose the direction of progression and transformation, if you are true to yourself, you can be what you elect to be—an enlightened being who can provide wondrous service to your world and all who are part of that world. Or you may choose to be merely one of a mass of units in embryo, drifting from one phase of existence to another in unintelligent indifference. Again, I ask you, Columbus, *what is your choice?*"

Agape's words reverberated throughout my being like rolling thunder. Undoubtedly, this was a powerful moment of truth for me. I was well aware that an impertinent response would be disrespectful to the sincerity of my communicator. On some deep, inner level of consciousness I realized this decision was something I had been unconsciously seeking for a long time. I couldn't explain how I knew, but I *knew*. In rapt thought, I pondered the essence of what I had presently comprehended. The energy of Agape's love was stimulating—but not compelling—me to aspire to a greater goal. I had no thought of time as I reflected on the adventure beckoning me to the unknown.

Finally, after a moment of tense stillness—a moment in which my heretofore life as Columbus Clam detached from me so that it seemed like a palpitating creature on the sea floor—a sob broke unconsciously from between my shells. Imploringly I searched for Agape. There was no response. And then, I suddenly found the very foundation of my own actual being. Hesitating no longer, I extended my foot and thrust myself forward. "In all of creation, there is no cause for fear," I felt myself exclaim as I plunged forward in the water.

A meteoric luminance pierced the blackness. I retained sufficient consciousness to wonder at its brilliancy. The Great Ocean at my feet became a heaving mass of swirling waters flocked with foam. I surrendered to the turmoil within me and the turmoil of the Great Ocean. Everything swirled into darkness and silence.

Gradually, I became aware of my surroundings again. A delicate warm glow was putting a gentle pressure on my shells.

"Rest, dear Columbus. You have done exceedingly well."

My sensations were exquisite. A fresh and radiant life poured itself through me. I was content to remain a passive recipient of such an inflow of well-being. I experienced no desire to move or to speak. Every trouble, every concern, every fear, every difficulty had passed from my mind.

"Agape, am I transformed?"

The warm glow intensified.

"Not yet. You are on the threshold. You have almost conquered your ego, but not quite. Now, the real work begins"

"Almost! Only 'almost'!" I groaned aloud and sank

lower into the sand of the sea floor, wondering and waiting.

Nothing happened.

When the tension became unbearable, I called out, "Agape, what do I do now?"

"Columbus, look within. What is your soul's sincere desire?"

"I want to let my light shine!"

"What do you perceive as the next step you need to take to accomplish this desire?"

There was something quite grand in the silence of the next few moments. A faint voice from within whispered, "The only difficulty may lie in the practical application of what you have learned." I listened. Nothing more was forthcoming. Suddenly, I *knew*. Mine was the upward and onward path! My next question? How do I find the great Coral Reef!

The Coral Reef 6

SOMEWHERE IT HAS BEEN stated that "the call compels the answer." This is true. How can I describe to you my journey to the Coral Reef? With great difficulty! Some energies of the mind and heart are not easily put into words.

I recall experiencing a burst of enthusiasm at the moment I made the decision to find my way to this special place, the Coral Reef. I also remember the clamor caused by numbers of reckless, scared, and stimulated creatures of the sea who were rushing hither and yon toward an indeterminate destination.

All of this activity, combined with the turbulent waters of the churning sea, created a blur of sound and movement. Eventually, I found myself in the most wondrous place and circumstances.

The Coral Reef was an underwater barrier ridge built of fragments of coral, coral sands, and solid limestone a few feet below sea level. I later learned this particular barrier reef was separated from land by several lagoons twenty to thirty feet deep. The reef thrived here; strong wave action aerated the water, supplying an abundance of food and oxygen, as well as preventing silt from accumulating and suffocating the coral.

The sea floor, which was fairly flat, was composed of sand, mud, and rock particles that had been formed by erosion and volcanic activity on land and then washed to the sea. The water temperature was ideal.

With a deep, restful sigh, I began to observe my surroundings. The Coral Reef was alive with a multitude of sea creatures! The reef apparently was home to several kinds of crustacea. Pairs of large, brightly colored shrimp were tucked into crevices in the reef. I observed a female crab settled in a notch of branching coral. Perhaps among the most spectacular life on the reef were the numerous beautiful fish, whose names I learned later: the large parrot fish, damsel fish, and cleaner fish. The poisonous species of stonefish, lionfish, and the moray eels darted about.

"Well, hello. How are you doing there, Little Fellow?" boomed a huge voice over my head.

I almost popped right out of my shells.

"W-w-what?"

"Welcome to the Coral Reef. I gather you are part of the 'newcomer' group of sea folk who are arriving to learn about *The Keys of Opportunity*."

I didn't see anyone as close as the voice sounded. "Who are you? Where are you?"

"My name is Tridama. I'm on the coral ledge slightly to your right, about three feet upward."

I directed my attention toward that area. All three chambers of my heart thudded together, and the ganglia of my nervous system shuddered in shock. There above me sat the largest, most spectacular mollusk imaginable. This giant clam appeared to have shells almost three feet wide! Absolutely amazing! I gulped as astonishment caused my ciliary action to bring in an overabundance of water. I was speechless.

"And what is your name, my friend?"

There it was again. That word "friend."

"I am known as Columbus Clam."

"And what brings you to these waters?"

"I am on a journey to learn more about *The Keys of Opportunity* and acquire a better understanding of what is happening in our world."

"Indeed. And what do you think is happening in our world?"

"I-I really don't know, but Agape has been talking with me, and something inside directed me to come to the Coral Reef. All kinds of events have transpired . . . and here I am."

"I see."

"Do you live here?"

"Oh, yes. For a long time."

"Do you know what is going on?"

"Well, though I am but the humblest of students in these mysterious matters, I have had a few bursts of insight."

"Would you tell me what you have learned? And can you tell me how to find *The Keys of Opportunity?*"

Deep laughter rumbled across the Coral Reef. "You may search for *The Keys of Opportunity* in your own way and in your own time."

Well! That certainly wasn't a definite response, at least not the kind I had expected. And I didn't appreciate being laughed at by a total stranger, either.

"Take no offense, Little Friend. I would be happy to share what I have learned. What is your question?" He seemed to have read my thoughts.

Question! Singular question! I had dozens of questions. Where did I begin?

"Begin within your heart, Columbus."

"Agape! You're here!"

"Yes, Columbus. And Tridama is indeed a true friend. He has much knowledge and wisdom. Look within and bring forth your uppermost question."

I tried to sort through the jumble of new information racing around in my consciousness. Slowly, my thoughts arranged themselves, and one particular question stood uppermost in my mind.

"Can you help me understand what is *real*?"

Tridama was silent for so long that I thought he had failed to hear, or perhaps forgotten, my question. Just as I was about to repeat it, he replied.

"Well, Columbus, you certainly selected an interesting starting place! Things often are not what they seem. Sometimes they are actually hoaxes perpetrated by our limited senses and lack of knowledge. To learn more, we must first realize how little we know. The unknown before us may be a million times greater than what we now know, despite the many discoveries we have made and are presently making. The rate of discovery is accelerating. The more we learn about our world the more humble we should be, realizing how ignorant we have been in the past and how much more is waiting to be discovered."

As he divulged this heavy-duty information, Tridama's voice increased in strength. It was easy to hear his enthusiasm as he continued.

"Columbus, the Great Creator is the core principle of everything. To learn more about reality, we need to admit that we do *not* know everything and that we are *not* the center of the universe. We presently comprehend only a small portion of the mysteries, forces, and spiritual realities surrounding us.

"Egotism has been a major cause of many mistaken notions in the past. It has led many species to believe that their particular life form represented the ultimate of creation. Egotism is still our worst enemy. Only by becoming humble and willing are we able to learn more. Humility allows for a never ending thrill of diligent, rigorous research for accelerating progress and usefulness.

Progress can accelerate forever. Mysteries solved lead to even more mysteries. Forces still undreamed of are present within and around us.

"The world is incredible, Columbus. Just the fact that you and I are here, that the atoms of our bodies were once part of the stars, is almost incomprehensible. But we're making progress!"

Perhaps *he* was making progress, and I even felt a small surge in *my* personal comprehension.

Agape spoke next. "Columbus, remember what I shared with you about the importance of listening to others? You may think you are not retaining much of the information being presented, but you are going to remember more than you think. The truth of which Tridama speaks will impress its pattern on your consciousness, and you will be able to bring it forth at the proper time."

"Everything exists in the unseen before it is manifested or realized in the seen," Tridama said. "In this sense it is true that the unseen things are the real, while the things that are seen are the unreal. The unseen things are the causative factor; while the seen things are the effect. The unseen things are the eternal, and the seen things are the changing, the transient. On a cloudy day there may appear to be no sun; but we have faith that the sun is only hidden. However, if we lived in a place that was continually cloud covered, it might be more difficult to believe that a sun always spreads its radiance over the planet.

"Until we reach the point in consciousness where we attune our thought processes to perceive the kingdom of the Great Creator, we judge our environment, its peoples, yes, even our world, by appearances. And perhaps we miss a lot of important knowledge this way.

"The members of the High Council and other learned scholars from many walks of life have agreed that nothing can be separate from the Great Creator. It's true. If the Great Creator is infinite, then nothing *can* be separate from him. A part of the Great Creator is within you, and you are a part of the Great Creator. We are all citizens of the spiritual world and we are spirit from the day of our conception. Love, loyalty, patience, compassion, and nobility of purpose are values more real than tangible objects."

Although I didn't comprehend everything Tridama was saying, on some level I recognized that this was a conversation I would long remember. As I waited for Tri-dama to continue, I realized that a considerable number of sea creatures had gathered around our location in the Coral Reef. They exuded an air of deep interest and expectancy. I returned my attention to the giant clam who held a vast reservoir of wondrous knowledge.

"Can you tell me *why* we were created?"

"Maybe one purpose was to help accelerate the Great Creator's creativity."

What? The clam was talking in riddles. "Could you explain that statement, sir?"

"Well, I don't know about 'explain'; however, I am happy to share my thinking along this line. The truth is that we can apprehend only a few of the infinite aspects of the Great Creator's nature, never enough to form a comprehensive conclusion. Nature reveals something of the Creator. The golden age of creation is reached as the Great Creator reveals himself more and more to the intelligence of his creations. Yet, we cannot learn every-thing about the Great Creator by studying nature, be-cause nature is only a partial manifestation of the Great Creator."

I remembered that Agape had mentioned nature

previously. As that thought passed through my consciousness, I could hear Agape whisper, "Yes, Columbus, 'nature' can mean the essential character of a thing that makes it what it is. It can also be described as the essence, innate disposition, or inherent tendencies of a being. Some thinkers have also referred to 'nature' as the sum total of all things in time and space—the entire physical universe."

World. Planet. Universe. I certainly had much to learn. A narrow ray of intellectual understanding slowly filtered its way into my consciousness regarding those things that I had recently heard spoken of so frequently.

"But what about *me*? Or what about the clam community? Can we bring this discussion to a more personal level?" I was aware of Tridama's smile as well as the supportive noises from the other sea folk gathered around. "Columbus, I believe you have heard the wave analogy. However, I would like to repeat it for your benefit and that of the others who are here. A wave is part of the ocean, and has no existence apart from the larger body of water. The wave is temporary, whereas the Great Ocean is relatively permanent. Each wave is different from every other wave. It is created by the ocean and is a child of the ocean. When it dies, it returns to and continues to be a part of the surging ocean that is continuously creating new breakers on the beach.

"For its duration, that wave is alive, having been created just as you and I were created. Like us, it consists of millions of atoms and cells. It lives, grows, dies, and hopefully produces after its kind in the process. Yet the wave cannot describe us. It has no ability to comprehend us or to understand the complexity of the culture of which it is a part. The difficulty a wave would have in describing a clam can be likened to our difficulty in describing the Great Creator. These musings are all a part of the mystery of life.

"You see, Columbus, the more knowledge we gain, the greater our perception of the unknown may become. There is no absolute definition of why you or I or any other creature was created. Those who dwell in three dimensions can comprehend only a small part of the Great Creator's multitude of dimensions. We search for additional bits of information and further our awareness as we progress along the journey of life."

Not a creature moved or spoke for quite a while. We were, in our individual ways, trying to absorb the wisdom of Tridama's words. One by one, we became aware of a powerful presence in our midst. Still, no one moved or spoke, and an unusual and powerful message resonated throughout the whole area of the Coral Reef. It seemed a miracle was worked in the heart of each one present.

> *The beginning traveler is one*
> *who has achieved a readiness for something new.*
> *This precious one has awakened*
> *from the deep slumber of the soul.*
> *This wondrous work of the Great Creator*
> *would now come apart from the masses*
> *and seek for himself.*
> *He has begun to awaken the sleeping mind.*
> *He has begun his own journey*
> *into the valleys*
> *and over the mountaintops*
> *of the Great Ocean.*
> *He has begun a new day.*
> *He is ready for himself.*
> *He is ready for life anew.*
> *The old way is no longer adequate.*

He would drink deeply
  of the Eternal Spring of Wisdom.
He would become uplifted
  and transformed.
He would become a willing servant
  to journey alongside others
  into the Heaven World,
  where joy awaits.
Come, my children,
  arise with me!

Resonance 7

WITHIN A SHORT TIME, I became a temporary resident in the Coral Reef community. After arriving there, and especially after experiencing the power that enveloped each one present when Tridama completed his dissertation about reality, a wonderful enthusiasm filled my being. The same enthusiasm was reflected in the countenances of many of the sea folk in the reef area.

Various ones met in small groups for discussions regarding the multiplication of mysteries we were all experiencing. At one point, I caught portions of a lively debate between Rigidity Clam and Researcher Clam. (My names for them, of course, are based on perceived elements of their intense personalities.) I was somewhat surprised to find that they had also traveled to the Coral Reef. But, then, why not?

For the first time since the experience had begun, I truly felt I was an involved part of this new community. I expressed my feelings to Tridama, who was perched on his favorite coral ledge.

"That's wonderful, Columbus. Perhaps you have begun to realize that no soul on this earth is completely alone. Life offers a duality. It is like half a shell that seeks the other half, and becomes dissatisfied and restless until it attains its object. In reality, each one is already complete, although the two halves may certainly be considerably effective when working together."

I speculated vaguely on the meaning of these words but was disinclined to ask more questions. There are no proofs as to why such things should be, but that they are is indubitable. The miracles taking place at this time in our history may sometimes be silent ones, but they are worked in the heart and mind of each individual who seeks greater heights of discovery. Some do not believe and may say, "Give me a positive sign. Prove clearly to me that what you say is true and I, in spite of my *string* and *quark* scientific theories, may believe." A response to

86

such a request was spoken about two thousand years ago: "Seek first the kingdom of heaven and all other things shall be added unto you."

I sincerely desire to allow my personal experiences to speak for themselves. If they seem somewhat strange, or even impossible, I can only say that the things of the invisible world may appear so to those whose thoughts and desires are centered only on this physical life.

The day that eternally changed my life arrived in natural splendor. The azure waters around the Coral Reef were deliciously warm and refreshing. Sunlight dappled the sea floor and reflected off the brilliant colors of the various sea creatures who assembled to share their new insights. What extraordinary gatherings and communications had occurred over the past few days!

Several of those in the reef area had traveled long distances, drawn by an unexplainable compulsion to learn more about *The Keys of Opportunity*. The quality of the exchange of ideas was amazing. Focused listening to the discussions brought a realization there are many names for the Great Creator: the Creative Source, The One, Divine Being, Eternal Love, Supreme Principle, and even the name, God. Everyone listened courteously to an extensive assortment of concepts and asked excellent questions that invited further exploration of a variety of subjects.

In the midst of an exciting discussion about the possible message of *The Keys of Opportunity*, Tridama paused abruptly in midsentence. As he turned to face the far end of the Coral Reef, even *he* appeared astonished. In one swiveling movement, all those present looked in the direction of Tridama's startled gaze. A hush ensued.

Lo and behold! What a wonderment to the senses appeared before us. We found ourselves looking into a shimmering wall of rainbow-colored sea creatures. There were blues, greens, soft mauves, tricolors, and some irregular patterns of color that could serve as camouflage. Someone commented that we were actually looking at a school of the showiest denizens of the sea, angelfish! Although angelfish usually swim singly or in pairs, this company of remarkable beauty moved in rhythm, all as one unit. There were emperor angelfish, blue-faced angelfish, French angelfish, and the exotic majestic angelfish.

While everyone's astonished attention was riveted to the spectacle before us, and just when an additional surprise did not seem possible, it happened! The shimmering "wall" began to part in the middle and the largest, most stately angelfish one could imagine swam slowly toward our group and seemed to hang suspended in the water before us.

"Greetings to each of you. And welcome to the Coral Reef. I know you are here because you have felt the call from some deep inner aspect of your awareness and have traveled to learn more about *The Keys of Opportunity*. We are here to assist you in the achievement of your desire; however, there is first some work that must be accomplished.

"Before you can comprehend what is truth, you must first understand what is not! Before the builder of a home can proceed with construction, he must clear the site of obstructive debris. He who would build his home from a true God-idea must, likewise, clear his mind of false conceptions and beliefs. Most of you have sincerely been involved in this process for a considerable time—although you may not realize that. In reality, your journey began from the moment the still, small voice began whispering to your partially sleeping consciousness."

Immediately my thoughts turned toward Agape.

"You are here because you have chosen to move through the wilderness in your consciousness where, for a time, you may have felt lonely and comfortless. This decision has allowed you to rid yourself of inaccurate conceptions and perspectives that may once have been quite useful but that no longer assist you in realizing greater truth.

"You are now moving in accordance with the Great Creator's love, which enfolds even the smallest portion of his creation. 'Many are called, but few are chosen.' Not all souls choose to become pure enough to succeed, without hindrance, in entering a greater awareness of *The Keys of Opportunity*. They will have another opportunity to learn, for the Great Creator leaves no one out. It must be remembered that, however great the number of those who seek to attain happiness in the Great Creator's presence, they form only one drop in the mighty ocean of life.

"If you are ready to proceed, we will escort you to the entrance of the Sanctuary Cave wherein *The Keys of Opportunity* await the sincere seeker."

As if on a strong invisible cue, the shimmering wall of angelfish turned in unison and began swimming toward the far end of the reef. Without a thought, I followed them. As we approached the entrance to the Sanctuary Cave, the wall of angelfish separated, with one-half of the group flanking either side of the cave's entrance. The giant angelfish remained suspended between the door of the Sanctuary Cave and the small group of sea creatures. For whatever reason, not everyone in the Coral Reef area had chosen to come to the Sanctuary Cave. A soft radiance effused from the entrance to the cave and encompassed each individual in a unique way. The angelfish leader began to speak.

"Precious ones, relax where you are for a moment. Think of the still, small voice that helped you reach this point of your journey. Feel the love that vibrated between you and this inner voice. Recall the name by which you recognize your personal assistant. Bring this name to the center of your heart."

Agape!

"Feel the essence of pure love glowing ever more brightly within you, bringing a comforting warmth. This love can transmute the last residue of old hurts, misconceptions, and egotistical ignorance into greater awareness and understanding. It can help you release any emotional remnants of guilt or shame. And this love can invite the larger warmth of the Great Creator's *Unlimited Love* to dwell with you eternally. When you use pure love in your daily activities, you have the ability to dissolve disharmony in your world."

As I focused on what the giant angelfish was saying, I had the impression that Agape's presence was infiltrating my every atom.

"Agape?"

"Yes, Columbus?"

"You're here! I haven't heard you for several days and wondered where you were."

"I've been with you all along, Columbus, listening to your conversations with others and basking in the expanding light of your consciousness. I am your special guardian, Columbus. I have been with you from your very beginning, and I can always communicate with you as long as your soul seeks spiritual enlightenment. Wherever you may travel, there am I also."

Agape paused for a moment. Then he chuckled.

"Do you remember what a difficult time I had in getting your attention when you were such an egotistical, self-centered clam?"

"That seems like a lifetime ago."

"It was, Columbus. Now is the beginning of life anew for you. Come with me."

The questions of my mind and heart were stilled. Speculations were dismissed. I was reaching past words, past thoughts, and it seemed as if I reached into the vast, loving heart of the Source of all there is. My own heart felt itself literally pressed to that of the Great Creator and it responded to the universal rhythm of love. An even deeper sense of joy enfolded me. All my clam things turned to mist. At the moment, they were remote, like animate shadows without substance, capable of being refashioned and transformed.

With tranquil satisfaction, I realized a process change was taking place in my consciousness. I did not *think* it. I did not *analyze* it. However, I did pursue it and *feel* it deeply as one who, listening to a wondrous symphony, sees the musicians who are incidental to the profound sweep and portent of the music they evoke.

How confident I felt. How ably I could cope with any situation. How mutable were those things that once seemed adamant in my life. In that moment, I called forth into the shadow world the sense of the eternal love of the Great Creator that would provide substance and reality. I made of my heart a chalice from which I could continually quaff the life essence of truth. And I expounded in overwhelming thankfulness!

An enormous burst of light flooded throughout my consciousness as I became a participant, as well as an observer, in a magical, unfolding drama. I suddenly realized I was *inside* the Sanctuary Cave of *The Keys of Opportunity*! Inexplicably, in that moment, I remembered something Tridama had said earlier. "When the Reality of Life is correctly understood, you may find that manifestations that now seem miraculous to you will be as natural and normal as swimming in the Great Ocean is to its inhabitants."

Well, I wasn't at that point in awareness yet. I was still searching!

I became aware of a chamber of extraordinary shape and remarkable beauty—a large, circular room that rose to a magnificent dome. The Sanctuary Cave appeared to be at least sixty to seventy feet in diameter. The walls were made of a dazzling white, transparent substance that glowed with a soft mother-of-pearl essence. As I became oriented to the room and could more easily focus my senses, I was able to see mathematical symbols imprinted in the wall.

At that moment, a vibration reverberated around the Sanctuary Cave. My heart chambers thudded. What was happening now? The vibration increased in intensity until I thought my shell would crack into a dozen pieces. A sound caused me to look toward the ceiling. What I beheld was incredible! A huge, luminous sphere was slowly descending to the floor of the center of the cave. I instinctively and immediately became aware of the presence of a powerful capacity of truth and light that had to be *The Keys of Opportunity*!

I felt myself being lifted, rising to meet and join with the most astonishing energy imaginable. I could not move or cry out. I could only feel that I was advancing steadily, breathlessly toward the sphere of light. Everything around me was lovely, refined, and perfected. I know not the words to describe this experience. A long, quivering flash of radiance, like a fragment of a rainbow, struck dazzlingly across my sight. This light was exquisitely pure and brilliant. Completely aware of my sensations, I seemed to be at *home* in some familiar element.

A voice from everywhere murmured musically, "Look

well, Columbus Clam, upon what shall be shown unto you, and listen with the intentness of your heart to the message that shall be given to you. Investigate everything miraculous and glorious that shall befall you. Reach with the utmost of your abilities to grasp the majestic reality and perfection of truth and wisdom. Guide yourself by the delicate spiritual instinct within you that affirms that with God all things are possible. You may share what shall be given, but make no attempt to convert others to your way of thinking. That is not your task.

"Now, let us begin . . ."

Wisdom from
The Keys of Opportunity 8

HAT I PRESENT TO YOU as *Seven Immutable Truths* represents the nucleus of the instruction gleaned from my meeting with *The Keys of Opportunity*. It is important to share with you, Dear Reader, that *The Keys of Opportunity* are not a destination, or an ending. Rather, they are thresholds to opening doors to growth. They are not something you want to, or can, possess; instead, you *invite* them to occupy your attention. They are a means of journeying further from any restrictive egotism, to explore additional universal concepts, and to discover even greater mysteries! My perceptions and perspectives regarding the elements of this outer life have changed considerably since this story began. I now realize there is no more important goal than to reflect the inner joy of the Great Creator's love expressing itself through each of us. A feeling of usefulness, stemming from an increasing awareness of my oneness with all of life, has become my place of eternal enthusiasm as well as a springboard for accelerating research. Ever present is the deep joy of our complete helpfulness as spiritual beings in a spiritual universe. Now, after a diligent search, I offer such "Truths" to speak for themselves.

You Are Not Alone

Is life visible to humans as a random accident, or is the universe in some way designed to produce life? Are there infinite worlds both like and unlike this world of ours? Given an abundance of matter and the uniformity of nature, could the same physical processes that led to the formation of the Earth and its solar system be repeated elsewhere? These are questions that have circulated among the great minds of the sciences, philosophies, theologies, and governments of our world. No thoroughly verified answer has been forthcoming. The part of the universe that is visible appears infinite in all directions, not only above in the larger cosmos, but also below in the most minute aspect of creation. In addition, in various ways, we realize that the whole is greater than the sum of its parts.

Our universe is progressing toward increasingly elaborate states of matter, energy, and forces more highly integrated than we may presently comprehend. That which is possible in nature tends to become realized. There is an orderliness of progression, endowed with an assurance of development but with a certain openness as to its possible forms.

Evolution may be full of surprises. Is the Great Creator only the arbiter and creative principle of the entire sweep of creation, from the Big Bang theory through the formation of star systems, to the origin and progress of creativity, love, purpose, intellect, and worship on at least one planet in one solar system? Also, are all of these only aspects of divinity?

The new horizons include not only the universe without, but also the universe *within* each of us. A study of our spiritual nature may well open up an infinity of discovery beyond our wildest expectations. Why is nature intelligible to us? When we observe nature, do we see the material phenomena rather than the underlying laws of physics? Why does the physical world seem to be a rational arrangement of things? How do we account for the layer upon layer of order lying hidden beneath the surface of everyday phenomena? Look at the example of expanding consciousness that transpired within my small world! My story began with one very egotistical clam who thought he was the ultimate in his existing world. Now, I consider my body and mind to be sacred and ever-changing configurations of energy waves and particles designed by the Great Creator as a temporary habitat for one most appreciative clam!

My experiences confirmed that I was not alone. Nor are you alone. Open your consciousness and look around! See what is before you.

Are You Divine?

Every form of nature is unique! No clam, or dolphin, or angelfish is exactly like its counterpart. Can you imagine a billion unique forms expanding, growing, and vibrating their life forces far beyond the normal range of consciousness? Does each individual play its personal note in the universal symphony of life? Is every note somehow necessary to the whole, and would it be missed were it not sounded? My experiences have taught me that the important thing to retain is an understanding of our own uniqueness and effectiveness as a divine creation of the universe. Even though we are not the whole, the whole certainly wouldn't be the same without us.

Are we part of a larger symphony of life that extends to infinity? And yet can we be consciously aware that each part is needed and is gently connected to every other part?

As we come to understand our own spirit, soul, and body to a greater degree, can we also learn why we respond the way we do to others and to situations in our realm of existence? Whenever a discordant experience may come into our consciousness, we have the ability to alter the situation. We are not helpless victims. We may take any situation into our consciousness and place it on the inner altar of the Great Creator's love.

Is the Great Creator the source of divine harmony? Is it within you and is it within others? Do we carry with us an innate sense of the presence of the Great Creator and become inspired to think, feel, and do the things that maintain harmony and productivity? Our inner experience is more important than our outer experience. The accelerating discovery of new information requires diligence and enthusiasm. Balance can be achieved as we integrate the various aspects of ourselves.

When we remember our divinity, can we look at our world and all the life forms in it with a broad, generous, friendly, and loving spirit? Can we live each day and continue our evolutionary progress as we maintain an open mind and understand that no one person knows the totality of truth?

Are We Eternal?

The Creative Source is behind all creation. Are we created by, and within, the Source? The Source is divine; thus, are we also divine? And if divine, are we eternal? Therefore, at a time of transition, or releasing the physical body temple, do we reunite in the Source, so we do not die?

It is important to honor our natural cycles. Observe the great tapestry of the universe that is woven with a magnificent ebb and flow. This universe is pulsating like our own hearts and like the microcosmic atoms vibrating within us. If we can attune with the rhythm of life, then can we dance the greatest symphony? If we deny its pulse, then might we miss the essence of life's expression?

Life focuses around rhythms, changes, times of rest, and times of activities, growing, unfolding, and delving inward. What can we do *in this moment* to make life easier, happier, more productive, and worthwhile for all time? Can we act out the beliefs of our heart? The voice of the Great Creator is as loud as our willingness to listen. As we seek the message from each experience, we find opportunities at every step along the journey of life to savor the fruits of our labor, research, and devotion.

An important part of each individual is larger than our smallness, stronger than our weakness, wiser than we think, and braver than any fear. If there is a part of us that is of the earth (earthy), is there not also a part of us that is of the Spirit (spiritual), and thus divine? That which is the real of us can transform the unreal. All that is false will pass away. Spirit abides.

When the seasons of our life have fulfilled the gifts of the teachings they bear and are concluded, does one remaining lesson move beyond the variety of opinions? That lesson is: One unchanging life breathes in and out through us, in which all the seasons of life humbly come to resolution in accelerating creativity and intellect.

Can You Be a Co-creator with God?

Learning is a lifetime activity of vast importance. To learn that each of us can become a co-creator with the ultimate Source offers an astounding awareness and a glorious opportunity. The knowing voice of the Great Creator exists in each of us, but we tend to call upon it in a haphazard manner. The voice persistently nudges us in the direction of our highest good by way of the humble path that may sometimes confound the logical mind. Is law, or principle, inherent in the Great Creator's purpose for all his creations? The significance of the ordering principle seems to have become increasingly appreciated with the development theory of relativity.

The divine idea of order is the idea of flow and adjustment, and as this idea becomes established in our thought, can all aspects of our life—mind, idea, and expression— be in harmony with the universal Creative Love?

The genius of the universe created us and instilled a portion of that genius within each of us. When we dare to reach beyond our comfort zone in life and declare that a great dream may be being dreamed through us, do we allow the genius aspect of the Great Creator to do its perfect work? It is one thing to embrace greater possibilities and quite another to take the steps needed to bring them into fruition.

Are we not spiritual beings in physical form? Is our world essentially a spiritual world? Might the underlying controlling forces, or energies, be identified as spiritual *principles*? When, in cognition, we establish our spiritual unity with this spiritual essence, do we perhaps begin to "see with the eyes of spirit"? Do wondrous things then begin to happen in our life?

Let's encourage creative thinking within ourselves and others. Let's overcome feelings of timidity and throw our talents enthusiastically into a variety of experiences and personal encounters. *Let's believe in ourselves and others*—for the kingdom of heaven does not come with large signs to be observed. The kingdom of heaven—the realm of expanding consciousness, progress, and divine opportunity—is already in the midst of us. Is this a new frontier for further exploration: our own inner being, and our own innate divinity? Can forgetting our divinity, or turning away from it, create a sense of separation from the Great Creator? As we remember our oneness with the Supreme Source, can we move into the energy flow of creativity? To create is to cause to come into existence; to originate; to bring into being. Can we say that to co-create is to move in harmonious resonance with the infinite creative energy and partner the results?

Forgiveness Sets Us Free

The exploration of the Great Creator's universe may be in an infantile stage, a beginning voyage into the realm of the Spirit. This journey may follow the twists and turns of an amazing evolutionary process involving many diverse phenomena. One necessary element of progress that *The Keys of Opportunity* emphasized was *Unlimited Love*, and the forgiveness aspect of that Love plays an important role in overcoming obstacles.

One may ask why forgiveness is so important. Let's take a look at what it means. Forgiveness is an inclination to release, to give up resentment or the desire to punish. It is an activity of loving pardon. Forgiveness is a process of exchanging the false idea for the true and erasing error from mind and body and life. When we are no longer burdened by withheld forgiveness, we can move forward with a renewed sense of peace and love. We may not be able to change the circumstances surrounding a situation, but we *are* able to change the pattern of our thoughts. It is important to keep our thoughts in an open, positive, and progressive mode, for as we think, so we are!

If we can allow the real and imagined hurts and wrongs of the past to remain in the past, we are not compelled to endlessly reenact those experiences. Forgiveness does not mean excusing. We become genuinely free when our gift of forgiveness to another is, at the very same moment, a gift received in our own heart.

Discoveries and inventions are continuing at a vigorous pace. Who can imagine what may happen as this accelerates? Each discovery reveals new mysteries. The more we learn, the more we realize how ignorant we may have been in the past and how much more remains to be discovered. Strange as it may seem, it could be important to forgive our feelings of *ignorance*!

Forgiveness is about loving one's self enough to be honest, open-minded, and willing to move forward in life. It is about learning to be grateful, not only for our personal mistakes but for all our experiences, even though some may be painful. Forgiveness can be about knowing that although we experience pain, we don't have to suffer. The faith expressed through our gratitude for our challenges can help dissolve the appearance of negative circumstances as we look for the good in the situation.

Through giving and forgiving, the old ego-centered structures that may have built up over a lifetime can crumble. When that wall comes down, we are free to build healthy structures in our minds. When true forgiveness takes place, no scars are left, no hurts or thoughts of revenge remain; there is only healing. We are then free to help the power of the Great Creator do its perfect work through us.

Thanksgiving Is a Guiding Light

When we affirm truth with a conscious, deliberate, and powerful image of spiritual reality and bow our heads in recognition of the Divine, then we may alter any situation. That's a broad statement, but it is correct. Giving thanks to the Great Creator can provide believers with a strength that can raise them to new heights of performance and insight.

Thanksgiving may be called the Principle of Gratitude, with fear playing an opposite role. Gratitude enhances the open-hearted, genuine appreciation for what is wonderful in our life. Fear can be a constrictive force that—if we allow its entry into our thoughts—can move us from the stability and strength of our own power.

Thanksgiving may be like a prayer of knowing that the words we speak and the actions we take should be in harmony with the purpose of the Great Creator for the benefit of his children. By making a profound effort to be one with the Great Creator, will what we do in life have a far greater rate of success?

Remember that each of us is important. Everything we say, think, feel, and do is important! We are planetary citizens, a wonderful part of a magnificent whole. Isn't it tremendous that more of earth's inhabitants are awakening now to this awareness and to greater responsibility? Realities glimpsed from afar are often seen as ideals. When viewed from closer range, they become the practical necessities of the time. Are events swiftly carrying us toward further realizations with tremendous speed in this important period in cosmic history? Is now the hour when the clarion call goes forth, inviting all to be infused with the light of expanding consciousness, to be of good cheer, and to exercise good will? Is this the hour when opening one's eyes to immediate situations and experiences becomes a necessity? No longer need we grope in ignorance or egotism.

The Principle of Gratitude is an aspect of the universe that deals with the flow of energy. That is, as we give out energy, we receive the impact of the returning cycle. This works in every arena of life. This spiritual principle is continuously combining the expectations of the mind with the power of the heart. When we create a "mold" for something good in our lives, the power of thanksgiving becomes a magnet to draw greater good to us.

Do you want to have life and have it more abundantly? Do you want to be transformed and renewed? If you do, the activity of giving thanks is a powerful key. Thanksgiving opens the door to increased spiritual growth. And isn't this the energy we desire to program into our daily lives?

Love Is the Pathway Home

Love is the unifying, harmonizing power of the universe—the spiritual glue that holds everything together. The unlimited love of the Great Creator gives freedom to his creation for trial and error and innovation around the foundation of principle and consistency. This unlimited love may be the basic reality from which all else is only fleeting perception by transient creatures. And there is no situation that love cannot help or heal.

Love accents the completeness of life. It is the ever-present potential through which we can find fulfilling action or a harmonious attitude. Through unlimited love, we can enter the dimension of spiritual unity, wholeness, and maturity, where we can be united more closely with the Great Creator and those around us. The universe is not isolated from us, nor are we from it! God's love is expressed through all phases of creation.

One of the foremost qualities of the Great Creator's nature is his all-encompassing love. Can bringing the two sides of our nature together (the physical and the spiritual) be an ongoing creative endeavor that continually moves us in beneficial directions? If we neglect either the heights or the depths of our experiences in life, we may only stagnate. Bringing the two together by attending to the practical details of everyday life, our love can gather power and momentum.

I can now more fully understand my wonderful companion along this journey, Agape. Agape represents that unselfish love that gives unceasingly and expects nothing in return. It is the love that grows as you give it away! Agape is that holy, unconditional love the Great Creator provides for us regardless of our appearance, our social status, our financial assets, our level of intelligence, and even regardless of how unloving our actions may be sometimes. I shudder when I recall my obstinacy and egotism during my early association with Agape.

When we practice unlimited love, it becomes easier to love our enemies, to tolerate those who may annoy us, and to find something to appreciate in every being, place, and experience. The great paradox of unlimited love may be that it calls on us to be fully ourselves and honor our individual truth, while releasing self-centeredness and giving with nothing held back. Love, as with any other spiritual virtue, doesn't simply fall into our life as manna from heaven. Like an inquiring mind, it needs to be cultivated.

Have you ever experienced the feeling that you wanted to go home? Of course, when we travel on a vacation or a business trip, we may enjoy every moment of our travels and still anticipate the moment we will return home. What is "home" and the attraction that beckons us? Home is sometimes described as a dwelling place, the habitat that is our natural environment, and the place where something is, or has been, originated.

All of the above descriptions are attractive, for I have learned my *true* home is not restricted to a physical location. My true home is in the heart of the Great Creator. Love is the transport vehicle on the pathway to home. And it is impossible to give too much love!

It is one thing to talk about love and quite another to feel its impact at work in body, mind, and spirit! I would like to ask you some questions that have been in my thoughts from the moment of meeting with *The Keys of Opportunity*.

Would you like to improve all levels of your being and all aspects of your life? How would it feel to know you were making a real contribution to your world? Would you like to feel that because of you and your work someone's life was blessed? Or that the whole universe was positively amplified because you were a part of it?

Just think, octillions of atoms are ready and waiting for your direction! Are you willing to grow to meet your good and, in the growing, to be open to give and to receive?

Rejoice! 9

CELEBRATE DAILY the joy in my life! Open your eyes in the morning with the expectation of a joyous day ahead of you. Allow the magnificence and beauty of life's blessings to fill your heart to overflowing. The joy in your heart is to be used abundantly for the lifting up of yourself and all with whom you come in contact. Joy is a great healing energy. Overflow with good will.

It was most helpful for me to recognize that the ego that insists upon having its own way can be a destructive ego. The soul becomes ready, not by grandiose expressions or by waiting for something to happen, but by diligent effort and increasing humility. Learning self-control is a key to gaining mastery over our lives.

What is the cause for this great joy? The response is multiple, rather than singular.

It has been some time now since my experience with *The Keys of Opportunity*. There have been opportunities to reflect deeply on the amazing progression of events that preceded this meeting. When I ask what, in addition to the Seven Immutable Truths, remains uppermost in my consciousness, I must reply in this manner.

First, I learned the value of listening carefully, thoughtfully, and gratefully to everyone's concepts of the nature of the Great Creator and the purposes for his creation. To a large extent, the future lies before us like a vast wilderness of unexplored reality. The One who created and sustained this evolving universe through eons of progress has not placed those in this present moment at the tag end of the creative process. We are at the point of a new beginning. We are here for the future! Everyone has something of value to contribute. My prayer is to be eternally receptive to research and wisdom, however varied may be the sources. I have a deep desire to learn more about the Great Creator's purposes.

A logical "next" focus is to learn more about how to be a *helper* in the Great Creator's purposes. Certainly, my contributions may be humble, but so are those of the greatest intellectual minds. The Great Creator has given each of us a mind capable of creative activity in the ongoing expansion of the cosmos, which includes the expansion of our own souls. This creative process moves through our thoughts, words, and deeds to become manifest in our lives. The objects we build and the deeds we accomplish emanate from our thoughts and our words. We could ask these questions of ourselves: How useful is my life? What talents can I build or increase? How can creativity make my life more meaningful and worthwhile?

As sunlight is a creative source, so our love can be a creative source of new life and ideas. Is the Spirit of the Great Creator like the vast ocean, and are we the many beautiful forms of life supported by the waters? So, how can we learn to be helpers in the Great Creator's purposes? In addition to the gift of individuality that has been so generously provided for each of us, he has also given us the priceless gift of free will. Why are we the recipients of such a gift and, having the right of self-determination, what shall we do with ourselves and this power? Possibly, we are created to become helpers in the Great Creator's accelerating activity.

My heart's desire is to live a life of loving service, in whatever way unfolds, and become a blessing to those around me. Life without purpose is life wasted. I want to accomplish anything and everything within my ability. I know my life is determined not so much by the experiences it brings to me as by the attitudes I bring to life. Circumstances may color how we look at life, but we retain the ability to choose what the color shall be. I accept that responsibility. This may mean attempting to understand the minds and hearts of others and feeling the effect I may have on them. Empathy and compassion are qualities that can be practiced and improved.

Oh, the joy of it all!

My prayer, my friend, is that this little dissertation has provided some avenue of interest for you and, hopefully, some drop of inspiration encouraging you to be diligent and open-minded in spiritual research. If so, then I, Researcher Columbus Clam, am grateful for this opportunity and wish you "bon voyage!" throughout your personal journey!

Recommended Reading

Other books by Rebekah Dunlap

Breakthrough!   *Macro-Mind Power*

Cosmic Healing   *The Rainbow Connection*

Other books by John Marks Templeton

Agape Love: A Tradition Found in Eight World Religions

Discovering the Laws of Life

Evidence of Purpose: Scientists Discover the Creator

*The God Who Would Be Known: Revelations of the Divine
in Contemporary Science*

Golden Nuggets

How Large Is God? The Voices of Scientists and Theologians

The Humble Approach: Scientists Discover God

*Is God the Only Reality? Science Points to a Deeper Meaning
of the Universe*

Is Progress Speeding Up? Our Multiplying Multitudes of Blessings

Looking Forward: The Next Forty Years

Possibilities for Over One Hundredfold More Spiritual Information: The Humble Approach in Science and Theology

Pure Unlimited Love: An Eternal Creative Force and Blessing Taught by All Religions

Riches for the Mind and Spirit: John Marks Templeton's Treasury of Words to Help, Inspire, and Live By

Spiritual Evolution: Scientists Discuss Their Beliefs

The Templeton Plan: 21 Steps to Personal Success and Real Happiness

Worldwide Laws of Life: 200 Eternal Spiritual Principles

Worldwide Worship: Prayers, Songs, and Poetry

Research Prize

The John Templeton Foundation offers one prize of $3,000 each year for the most convincing article, of more than one thousand words, describing creative new research projects that might lead to one hundredfold more spiritual information.

All articles received by October 30 are eligible for the annual prize awarded on the following January 30. Please send completed articles to Paul Wason, *Possibilities for Spiritual Information Research Prize*, John Templeton Foundation, Five Radnor Corporate Center, Suite 100, Radnor, PA 19087.